MW00931529

Passover Story With Zombies

Telling the story of the redemption of the Jewish people from Egypt is the main Mitzva of Passover.
The Haggadah, the booklet which Jewish people read at the Seder dinner means in Hebrew "Telling". It is to emphasis the importance of telling the story from father to son.

The lesson of the four sons in the Haggadah is that each person needs to learn the story of the Exodus of the Children of Israel in a unique way. A way which is suitable for him or her.

Today kids are all into Minecraft, Facebook & Zombies..
They might not care about a story which happened 4000 years ago. Unless it includes.. Zombies.
For these kids this story of the Exodus is delivered with Zombies.

Author: Rachel Mintz
Illustrator: David Levin

Table Of Contents

Chapter 1 – Children Of Israel Move To Egypt

4000 years ago, a man called Israel and his children had to leave their land due to harsh famine. The large tribe of Jewish people moved from their land to Egypt, seeking food and water.

For a few years they received warm hospitality, and the King of Egypt respected them as guests.

But after the king died, the new king did not think of the Children of Israel as guests, for him they were foreigners in his land, and had to be enslaved.

For 400 years the Children of Israel could not leave!

On the throne was King Pharaoh which was so powerful he had thousands of slaves working for him building his mysterious pyramids. Children of Israel had been slaves for four hundred years, were working in hard labor from sunrise till sunset.

Chapter 2 - Pharaoh and His Zombies

King Pharaoh had sorcerers who looked into rising smoke and could tell him the future. He had Zombies in his palace who served him and obeyed him.

His sorcerers told him of a threat which is developing within his empire. They had seen in the smoke a few stars, but of these stars seemed to be shinning bright more than the others. They knew that a Jewish boy would be born, and when this kid will grow up, he will become the leader of the Jewish nation and will overturn the entire Egyptian empire.

Pharaoh decided to listen to his sorcerers advice and ordered the Zombies to make sure the Children of Israel will get harder work. But the Zombies said to him "Oh almighty king of the sun and winds, hard labor will not be enough!". "so what do you want me to do?" asked King Pharaoh.
The Zombies answered "all Jewish baby boys must be thrown into the Nile river".

Jewish baby boys must be thrown into the Nile river.

Chapter 3 - Moses is Saved

One Jewish family who heard the order of Pharaoh, decided not to give their baby to the grisly fate pharaoh planned for them.

The mother called her daughter and said to her "Each morning the princess of Egypt comes down to the Nile river to wash, she has a special pond where the waters are cool and clear. Take your baby brother before the sunrise and place him in a small basket near that pond". The sister listened her mother as the candle light shadows danced in the hut. The mother added " don't leave him there, stay and watch over him! God will protect the baby".

The daughter went and placed the basket in the Nile and watched it as it drifted into the shallow pond. She sat behind the reeds and watched.

When the princess of Egypt came to the Nile to wash, she was alone. While she prepared for her morning bath, she heard a baby laughter near by. She tried to find where the laughter came from.. She walked into the shallow waters and saw a small basket with a beautiful baby boy looking up at her.

She pulls the basket out of the water and calls the baby Moses*.

The princess of Egypt saves Moses and takes him

back to the Palace and raises him as her own. Without the Zombies knowing a Hebrew child is raised in their palace as the prince of Egypt.

*Pulling a boat or basket out of the water in Hebrew is called Masha, in the bible the baby is called Moshe.

God will protect the baby.

Chapter 4 – Killing The Egyptian

Moses grew up in the palace of the great Pharaoh. He hated being in the palace, as he saw dozens of horrible Zombies and Mummies walking and stalking the empty halls of the palace.

Moses toured around the land of Egypt riding his step father's chariots pulled by two black stallion horses. He saw the Hebrew slaves working in hard labor, preparing mud bricks, carrying sand and water, back and forth, being whipped by cruel creatures and Egyptian guards.

He could not bear to see the suffering of the Jewish people. One day as Moses was out in the vast plains of Egypt, he saw an Egyptian Zombie guard beating a Hebrew slave!

Without hesitation Moses jumps off the chariot and kills the Egyptian Zombie guard.

Once he understands what he has done, Moses decides to flee into the desert. He runs back to his black stallions and rides far into the wilderness. He knew he had to flee as far as he could, or his step father and his zombies will revenge the guard's life.

His journey ends after a few days in the land of Midian.

Chapter 5 – The Burning Bush

In Midian, Moses life changes dramatically. From a prince he becomes a shepherd for a man called Jethro. One day as he was out tending Jethro's sheep in the desert, Moses sees the most unbelievable sight he has ever seen!

He sees a large bush which caught fire, the fire was burning furiously but the bush in the middle of the fire DID NOT burn! It stayed green!

It was a sign from god, who called Moses and speaks to him from the burning bush.

God tells Moses that he has been chosen to free the Children of Israel from slavery in Egypt.

God reassures Moses that he is not sent to confront Pharaoh and the Zombies alone, because God himself is going to be there with him to free the people of Israel from Egypt, and Moses is his chosen messenger.

God tells Moses he should fear not, and agrees he can take his brother, Aaron with him.

As the astounded Moses retreats back to Jethro's tent camp, God's voice from the burning bush follows him through the desert "Go down to Egypt and tell Pharaoh to Let My People Go!" .

"Go down to Egypt and tell Pharaoh to let my people go!"

Chapter 6 – Moses and Aaron Come To Pharaoh

Moses and his brother Aaron came back from Midian to the land of Egypt.
They called Pharaoh and his Zombie advisers.
"The God of the Children of Israel has sent us, he has a message for you" they said.
"What is the message?" asked Pharaoh.
Moses said "**Let my people go**!" they declared.

But Pharaoh just laughed. Pharaoh knew nothing about the God of the Children of Israel and became very angry! He ordered his blood thirsty Zombies to make sure the Children of Israel work even harder than ever before. "From now on they have to make double amount of bricks" he announced.

Moses and Aaron were not frightened by Pharaoh or the Zombies!
They threatened Pharaoh if he will not obey the Lord, he will suffer 10 terrible plagues! Pharaoh's face became grim as he shouted "You will not threaten me in MY PALACE! Go away or you will be thrown to the deepest pit of snakes and scorpions!"

Moses and Aaron went away, the next day they came back with the same demand: "Let my people go!"

Chapter 7 – The First Plague - Blood!

Pharaoh dismissed their demand once again, and soon Moses and Aaron began to show him and his army of Zombies, the strength of the God of the Jews. Plague after plague soon struck the Egyptians, each one more shocking than the next.

Moses asked Aaron to throw his staff on the ground, and it turned into a snake! But Pharaoh asked his Zombies to do the same, and when their staff hit the floor, it turned into a snake too.
But Moses's snake, crawled over and swallowed the Zombie's snake. This got Pharaoh mad! He was humiliated. "I will not let anyone go!" he screamed.

Moses asked Aaron to touch the water of the Nile with the tip of his staff. As soon as the tip touched the water, the Nile river turned to blood! All the water in the Nile became red! Every pond, stream and drop of water in the land of Egypt turned into blood.

While Pharaoh was startled by the plague, his Zombies laughed! "This is nonsense!" said one terrible Zombie "we are not afraid from blood! We drink it like juice", and he sipped bloody water out of a clay cup, his lips turning red as he drank.

"we are not afraid from blood!"

Chapter 8 – The Second Plague - Frogs!

When Pharaoh saw the Zombies laugh, he did not want to show he was worried from Moses and Aaron threats..

So the next day when Moses and Aaron came back to the Palace, they were nearly killed.
"Go away, you two!" Pharaoh shouted and threw his spear toward them! Both of them dodged to avoid the spear swirling between them.
Moses straightened up, wiping the dust of his clothes, looked Pharaoh in his eyes, and claimed the same demand: "Let my People Go!"

Pharaoh saw the Zombies were watching his response. He did not want to look scared, so he said "NO! The Children of Israel are MY slaves, and no God can command me to let them go".

"It's your choice" Said Aaron and struck the floor of the palace twice with his staff.
As he did that, the water of the Nile began to bubble, and thousands of frogs began to leap out!
Ugly, shinny, lumpy, green frogs and toads leaped from the Nile river. Within a few hours millions of them swarmed every home and house in Egypt.

Pharaoh who despised frogs leaped himself from the

floor to his majestic chair. He sat there all day, watching the Zombies munching frogs like french fries, until the sun was down.

Ugly, shinny, lumpy, green frogs and toads leaped from the Nile river.

Chapter 9 – The Third Plague – Lice!

The day after Moses and Aaron came back.. with the same demand: "Let my People Go!"
Pharaoh who was disgusted from the frogs, still did not want to look weak in front of his servants, so he answered in a stern voice "I told you not to come back, my Zombies have eaten your frogs, and your people will stay here, as my slaves!"

Moses looked at Aaron, who looked back at him.
They shrugged and turned around, leaving Pharaoh and his Zombies puzzled.

"I told you they are whips!" said the head of the Zombies, and began to scratch his head...
As soon as Moses and Aaron left the palace, every one in the palace began to scratch their head. They were filled with lice!

Every person and creature in the land of Egypt was soon scratching their skin like madmen. The land of Egypt was covered with lice.

The land of Egypt was covered with lice.

Chapter 10 – The Forth Plague – Wild Animals!

A few days later, Moses and Aaron came back.
"Let my People go!" They said to Pharaoh. He was nearly bald, his hair was wary and his head covered with red deep scratches.

"No!" He said, as he thought the worst part was behind him.

Moses looked at the Zombies and said "OK, then the Lord almighty God of the Jewish nation will strike you again." They left the palace as silence fell on the rooms.

The floor began to rumble, Pharaoh rushed to the window and saw a huge cloud of dust, and heard a distant roar approaching.

Within a few minutes hordes of thousands of wild animals invaded from the desert and wilderness in to Egypt! They rushed and crushed everything in their pass. Destroying tents, huts, and crops.
Pharaoh ordered to close all the palace gates.
The Zombies were disappointed when the gates were shut, they planned to catch as many wild animals for their evil feasts.

Hordes of wild animals invaded in to Egypt!

Chapter 11 – The Fifth Plague – Sick Animals!

The next day when Moses and Aaron came, Pharaoh still did not want to let the Children of Israel go.

The next plague God has planned for Egypt, was sending deadly pestilence and diseases to strike the livestock and cattle in Egypt. Soon every horse, donkey, camel and goat, were dying in disease.

The Zombie plan to feast on the wild animals they caught was ruined! The wild animals became sick, their skin and fur crippled and shed. They were so gruesome to look at, everyone in the king's palace became sick.

Pharaoh was very distressed, all his cattle and livestock died! He had bought them in exchange for many gold coins and now they are all gone!

Sending deadly diseases to strike the livestock and cattle in Egypt

Chapter 12 – The Sixth Plague – Boils!

While Pharaoh was already willing to let the Children of Israel go free, God hardened his heart, as he had a few more plagues to show his strengh.

When Moses and Aaron came to the palace, Pharaoh moved in his chair uneasy, and said, "I don't mind the Children of Israel to go to the desert and worship their god, but then they must come back immediately!"
"No", said, Moses, "you must let them go free!"
Pharaoh did not like the sound of Moses voice. No one speaks to the king of Egypt like that!
And as god planned Pharaoh heart hardened. "If you do not accept my offer, forget about it – Your people will stay here!
His Zombies chuckling around with pieces of rotten meat dropping from their mouth.

God struck again!

This time every person in Egypt was covered with boils! A horrible skin disease which causes body parts to peel and fall off. Soon everyone in the land of Egypt looked like a Zombie. Scared and wary servants walked through the palace, king Pharaoh could not even look at them, as they were all disgustingly sick.

Every person in Egypt was covered with boils!

Chapter 13 – The Seventh Plague – Hail!

Pharaoh knew he was over powered by the God of the Hebrew people. His palace looked like a graveyard, filled with body parts and twisted people. But he just could not bring himself to admit he was defeated.

The next day, again, he refused to let the Children of Israel to go free! Moses raised both arms to the sky, and heavy clouds began forming above the palace.
Pharaoh eyes widened in fear, and even the Zombies were silent as the clouds became dark and the first drops of rain fell.
"That's it? a little rain?" Pharaoh laughed.

And as God heard him, the rain became heavier and harder, and hail began to pour on Egypt.

The hail was storming down like stones! Then the hail mixed with fire! Long lines of flaming rocks rained over the Palace of Pharaoh. Red hot rocks fell from the sky, destroying everything on the ground, causing fires and destruction.

Many of the Zombies which were outside died when they were hit by flaming rocks and ice.

"OK, OK! They can go!" screamed Pharaoh. But Moses and Aaron had already left.

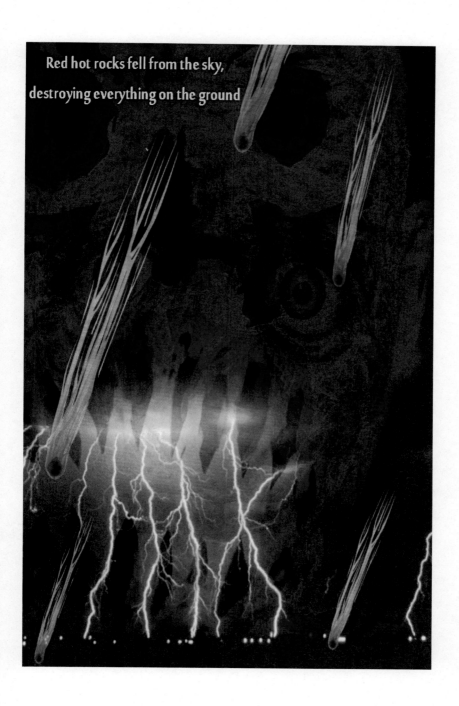

Red hot rocks fell from the sky, destroying everything on the ground

Chapter 14 – The Eighth Plague – Locusts!

By the time Moses and Aaron came back, God made Pharaoh heart hard as stone again.
"Your people can go to the desert for three days, then they must come back." Pharaoh tried to negotiate a deal with Moses.

Moses did not plan to negotiate when he knew God is behind him. So he just said "let my people – Go!"

When Pharaoh did not respond, God struck again!
Enormous swarms of locusts flew into Egypt. The skies became dark as many of them flew by. The locusts devours all the crops and greenery. Pharaoh was terrified from the famine which was expected after all the crops are consumed by millions of little hungry locusts pests.

The Zombies were waving their lengthy arms trying to avoid them. The locusts were all over the land, eating crops and leafs of every plant and tree in the kingdom.

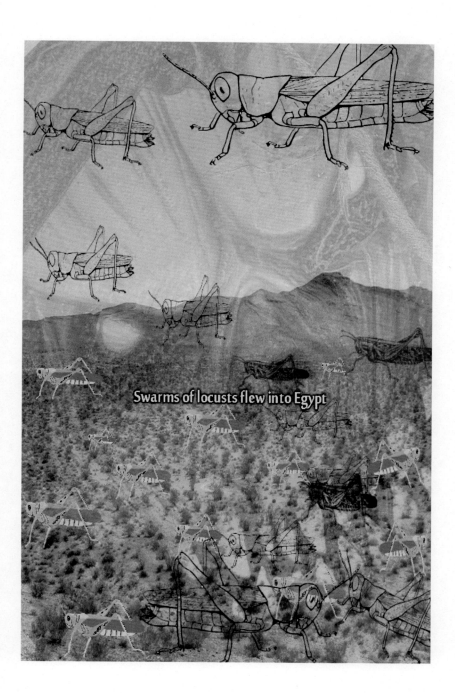

Swarms of locusts flew into Egypt

Chapter 15 – The Ninth Plague – Darkness!

When the swarms of locusts have left Egypt, the land was devastated. Not a single green leaf could be found on the trees, bushes and crops.

Moses came back to the palace, the next morning. The same palace he lived in as a boy. The king of Egypt was sitting on his high chair, his silk clothes torn, the golden crown pushed down on his forehead, and all his pride lost.

The zombies persuaded him not to let the Children of Israel go free, "They are your slaves! You can't be soft, or all the other slaves will want to break free too!"

"No!" Pharaoh answered to Moses as the same demand lay before him.

With god powers Moses pointed to the sky, and the clear blue sky began to turn in to dark blue, then to deep darkness, and then there was pitch darkness!

The Zombies were frightened!

Though they liked the darkness, it was too dark even for them. No one could see an inch further from their nose. They began to run and stumble and fall one on each other.

Soon screams of injured Zombies were taring the palace.

And then there was pitch darkness!

Chapter 16 – The Tenth Plague – Death of The Firstborn!

In total darkness Moses and Aaron came the next day to the palace. King Pharaoh and the Zombies could not see them but they surely heard their voice.
"Let the Jewish people Go! Said Moses in a low voice.
Pharaoh heard the threat in Moses's voice. He nearly said "yes" but a Zombie standing next to him, punched an elbow in his side.
"No one is leaving my kingdom!" Was the answer heard in the pitch dark room.
"Then you shall suffer!" Said Moses and left.

Moses went to the Children of Israel and told them to prepare to leave. They had to sacrifice a lamb to show their belief in God and smear the lamb's blood on each and every door post on their house. This would be a sign for the spirit of God which will pass through the land of Egypt that night to Pass-over their homes.

On that night the spirit of God struck the fiercest plague on the Egyptian king. The tenth plague, death to every firstborn!

The spirit of God passed over* the houses of the Jewish people, killing the firstborn of the Egyptians.
No matter if it belonged to an animal, servant , king or

Zombie. On this night Pharaoh's firstborn child was struck too. Every Zombie first born child was killed too.

*This is why this holiday is called Passover.

"Then you shall suffer!" Said Moses and left.

Chapter 17 – The Exodus - Freedom!

Finally, the next day Pharaoh had enough. He ran terrified in his palace, defeated, sorrowed and weak.
When he saw Moses he shouted "Go! and take all the Children of Israel with you, don't ever come back!"

The message was passed from one family to another. After 400 years of slavery, the Jewish people were free to go.
"Hurry! Hurry!" Moses urged them to leave.
He knew Pharaoh might change his mind at any moment.

The people of Israel told Moses, "we have to wait, we prepared dough for the bread.. we must wait till it is ready!" But Moses knew they had to flee in a hurry.
"No! Don't wait for your bread to rise, just go!"

The Children of Israel that day on the fifteen of the Hebrew month of Nissan left Egypt in such a hurry, carrying their belongings on their backs, and faith in their hearts. Their unleavened bread called Matzah stacked under their arms.

They didn't even look back to see the Zombies wondering in the streets looking for revenge on their dead firstborn children.

Chapter 18 – Crossing the Sea!

A few days later, Pharaoh regretted he allowed his slaves to leave. He called his army and the Zombies and ordered them to prepare to pursue after the fleeing people, and to bring them back!

The Zombies and the large Egyptian army formed long lines, and were led by Pharaoh in his chase after the people of Israel. At the third day, after constant marching, Pharaoh saw a cloud of dust over the horizon.
He knew that at that direction was the Red Sea, and soon the fugitive slaves will meet their fate, with nowhere to go. They will have the Red Sea in front of them and an army of thousands of Egyptians and Zombies behind them. They will have to surrender and come back.

The Children of Israel saw the huge army pursuing them, they saw the sea in front of them, they too thought they were doomed.

But God had other plans...

He ordered Moses to strike the sea with his staff. The Red Sea began to retreat and split into two. Walls of sea water began to pile on both sides. A path of dry land appeared!

The People of Israel were beholden by God's miracle, they cried in happiness as they began to run.

Not far behind them Pharaoh ordered his soldiers and Zombies "For the name of your king Pharaoh.. Go and bring them back!"

The Children of Israel saw the huge army pursuing them

Chapter 19 – Pharaoh & Egyptian Army Drown

As soon as Pharaoh and the army of Zombies charged forward and chased the Children of Israel into the split sea. The last of the Hebrew people had reached the other side.

At first the Egyptian army was sure it will overrun the fleeing people. But as they were in the middle of the dry path, the walls of sea water began to swell in. Within seconds bursts of sea water poured all over.
With gushes of water roaring around them, the Zombies and Egyptians tried to turn back and retreat. But it was too late..
The walls of water gave in, and the Tsunami tidal waves poured and drowned Pharaoh with his whole army of Zombies and Egyptian soldiers.

On the other side the people of Israel rejoiced. They witnessed one of God's most marvelous miracles with in their own eyes!

With gushes of water roaring around them, the
Zombies and Egyptians tried to turn back and retreat.

Chapter 20 – Reaching The Land Of Israel

Moses led the people of Israel through the desert, all the way to Mount Sinai. There the Children of Israel were chosen to get holy bible. Moses went up to the mountain and after three days came back with two huge tablets of rock with the Ten Commandments engraved into them.
Once the Children of Israel committed themselves to obeying God and the ten commandments, they knew the bond between them and the Lord is infinite.

But the journey was not over yet. It took 40 more years of wandering in the wilderness until they reached the place God promised them.

God led the people of Israel through the desert all the way to the land of Israel. The same land they left because of the famine.
After 440 years, the Children of Israel were back home.

The End

God led the people of Israel through the desert
all the way to the land of Israel.

Other books you might like:

Children Passover Fun Book

68 Pages of fun activities for children. Fun way to learn about Passover, Chametz, the Ten Plagues, Matzah and much more.. (Kindle + Paperback).

Seven Passover Songs Kids Should Know at The Seder

The Passover songs your kids need to know, translated and illustrated.

The 49 Days Of Omer Counting In Pictures.

The most beautiful way to learn and count the Omer. How to bless, and a full 49 colorful pages for each day. Plus a translated Hebrew phrase per day.

41440193R00027

Made in the USA
Middletown, DE
12 March 2017